To Saskia

Rabén & Sjögren Stockholm

Translation copyright © 1994 by Rabén & Sjögren
All rights reserved
Originally published in Swedish by Rabén & Sjögren
under the title *Den gamle musikanten*, text copyright © 1993 by Rita Törnqvist
Illustrations copyright © 1993 by Marit Törnqvist
Library of Congress catalog card number: 93-664
Printed in Belgium
First edition, 1994

ISBN 91 29 62244 1

Rita Törnqvist

The Old Musician

Illustrations by Marit Törnqvist

Translated by Greta Kilburn

R&S
BOOKS

Stockholm   New York   London   Adelaide   Toronto

In a cottage a short way from the village, behind
a hedge of green, lived a man and a woman.
They were old, but they still managed well.
They had two pairs of strong hands and a goat
and a kitchen garden. When the day's work was
done, the man played for his wife on a wooden
flute that he had carved himself.

One beautiful spring evening, as he sat playing by the open window, a blond little girl emerged from amid the greenery. She stopped to listen by the gate. The man laid his flute down beside him.

"Please keep playing!" said the child.

"Why don't you come in, instead," said the man, and he walked down the garden path to meet her. "Where do you come from?"

"From the village," she said. "There was such a lot of noise at home, and here the birds were singing. And suddenly I heard you …"

"My dear girl," said the woman, and gave her a glass of milk and a freshly baked roll. "When you finish eating, we will take you home."

And the little girl walked down the green path in the dusk, as the old man played his flute for her.

"It's as if you are talking to the birds," said the girl, and she skipped along next to him.

He trilled and chirped on the flute until they reached the village.
Then he took the girl by the hand and said, "Now it's your turn to
show me the way."

She led him down a narrow street and stopped in front of a shop window full of musical instruments. The shop door opened and a man came out with a long, narrow case that ended in a bell.

"Good luck with it," said the music-shop owner, and briefly watched his customer go down the street. "Child, where have you been?" he said when he saw the girl. "I was just about to go and look for you." He picked up his daughter and carried her inside.

"I want you to play for me again!" said the girl to the old man over her father's shoulder before the door closed behind them. But he walked home silently in the twilight.

After that evening, the old man always sat by the window when he played his flute. He played a little longer every day and let weeds grow among the vegetables. He forgot to fetch wood and all his melodies were full of a strange longing.

One early morning when he was going to the village for supplies, he told his wife that he would be back later than usual. His wife stood at the gate for a long time looking after him. The flute was sticking out of his knapsack.

The old man hurried to the village and quickly found the street where the little girl lived. But when he saw her there playing marbles with some other children, he turned down a side street leading to the main square. He sat down on a bench under an old linden tree and ate some bread from his knapsack. Then he took out his flute and played until the little girl came skipping over to him across the square.

"I have been waiting for you," she said. "I have tried out all the flutes in the shop, but not one of them sounds as nice as yours."

"Then I'll teach you to play mine," said the old man, and he showed her how he put his fingers on the holes. She did as he had done and played a clear note. Next he taught her a simple melody, and neither of them noticed that people were stopping to listen. They did not look up until the innkeeper came out and said:

"Listen, old musician, would you play for my customers tonight?"
The old man nodded, surprised. But that evening at the inn he
played in vain.

"Blow a bit harder," whispered the innkeeper in his ear, and gave him a glass of beer.

The old man played his flute as loud as he could, but people walked in and out without paying attention to his music.

Then the innkeeper gave him a long wooden tube that ended in a funnel.

"This is a shawm," he said. "It is older than you and me put together. If you play this, everyone will hear you."

As soon as the old man started to play on the shawm, people turned toward him.

"Sit on the table, musician, so we can all see you!" they called out.

The old man played until his lips were numb, and still they wanted him to continue. "No, that's enough," said the innkeeper. "You'll have to come back tomorrow."

Early the next morning, the little girl went to the inn. She heard shrill sounds coming from the bar and peeked in. She saw the old

man practicing on a strange instrument, and she walked away, disappointed.

From that time on, shawm music was played at the inn every night. People tapped their feet in time with the music. The bar was packed and there was a line outside the door. The town's bandmaster didn't like to see so many people going to the inn to listen to music. He proposed that in the future the musician should play in the town pavilion, in the middle of the park. There everyone would be able to hear him. The innkeeper promised to serve refreshments.

The old man's cheeks bulged as he played in the round pavilion, but the bandmaster was surprised to discover that the shawm sounded softer there than he had hoped.

"I'm sorry," he said, "but you cannot be heard all over the park. We'll have to buy you a different instrument."

Everything was a mess in the music shop when the two men entered. The girl's father was packing crates and boxes.

"Are you leaving the village?" asked the old man, startled.

"We are moving to the capital next week," said the shopkeeper. "Business is bound to be better there. Was there anything you wanted?"

"This musician is looking for an instrument that can be heard all over the park from the pavilion," said the bandmaster, and pulled a copper horn out of a box.

The old man started to play softly on it, and the two men nodded approvingly.

It was not long before the warm sounds from the horn filled the entire park. People flocked in to listen. But one little girl went home.

The old man lowered the horn slowly, and there was a burst of applause which did not stop until the bandmaster mounted the stage and said:

"I propose that we have our old friend take part in the King's annual music competition in the capital, on behalf of the village."

The audience cheered and applauded, and the old man looked surprised and nodded.

Sometime later he and his horn left for the capital, which had been built on the slopes of a mountain. At the top, a palace with hundreds of windows glittered in the sunshine.

At the bottom was the square where the music competition would be held. It was vast, and it was so crowded and so busy that the old man had to elbow his way through the throng.

What am I doing here, he thought when he reached the other side. And he escaped into a side street. There his eyes fell on a sign with a huge wind instrument on it — a big copper circle with a broad bell. The legend read "Music Shop Helicon" in elegant lettering, and the actual instrument was displayed in the window.

"He-li-con, he-li-con," the old man repeated twice and kept staring until the door of the shop opened. He looked up and saw the father of the little girl who had sold him the horn.

"How can I be of service to you this time?" said the shopkeeper with a smile.

"I … I have promised to take part in the music competition," said the old man, stammering. "But I fear that I am not up to it."

"The sound of your horn is probably too delicate," said the shopkeeper. "But wait a moment." He walked to the display window and took out the helicon.

Just then the sound of small feet was heard on the stairs and the little girl ran into the shop.

"Where is your flute?" she asked, and looked expectantly at the old man.

Hesitantly, he pulled the flute out of his knapsack, and she began to play a tune on it that she had learned from him.

Her father looked at her with surprise.

Then he smiled and said to the old musician: "We can swap if you like. You get the helicon and she keeps the flute."

The old man swallowed a few times and nodded.

"You can practice in the valley north of the city," said the shopkeeper, draping the enormous instrument over the old man's shoulders.

It was not easy for the old man to
master the helicon. But when he
finally heard the sounds bounce
back and forth between the
steep mountainsides, he
began to long to let
them flow out over
that immense
square.

The entire city turned out for the competition. Musicians had come in droves from all parts of the country. They played the most curious instruments, which did not always sound in tune. None of them was loud enough.

The old man with the helicon was the last person to play. A hush fell over the crowd when he appeared on the stage. He filled his lungs slowly, then put his lips to the mouthpiece and let a mighty melody roll over the vast square. When the last warm notes disappeared, the crowd was silent, waiting breathlessly until the King himself got up to speak.

"The silence has spoken," he said.

The cheers that soared from the square made the old man feel as if he and his helicon were being lifted up to the sky.

"And now the prize!" said the King, and he pointed to the top of the mountain. "The palace that has as many windows as there are days in a year! You may live there for one year. For each day, there is a window with a new, breathtaking view."

"Me, live there?" said the musician, faltering.

"One whole year," said the King. "And please save the windows in the towers for the very last."

The King personally took the winner to the palace. In the large bright hall, a row of servants bowed, and on the table in the dining room a banquet awaited them. When they finished eating, it was already night.

"But, your Majesty," stammered the old man. "Why don't you live here yourself?"

"My palace is down in the city, among the other houses," said the King. "Up here you can play to your heart's content and we will all enjoy your music."

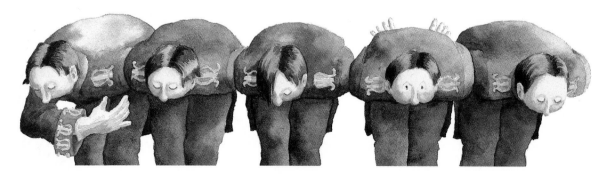

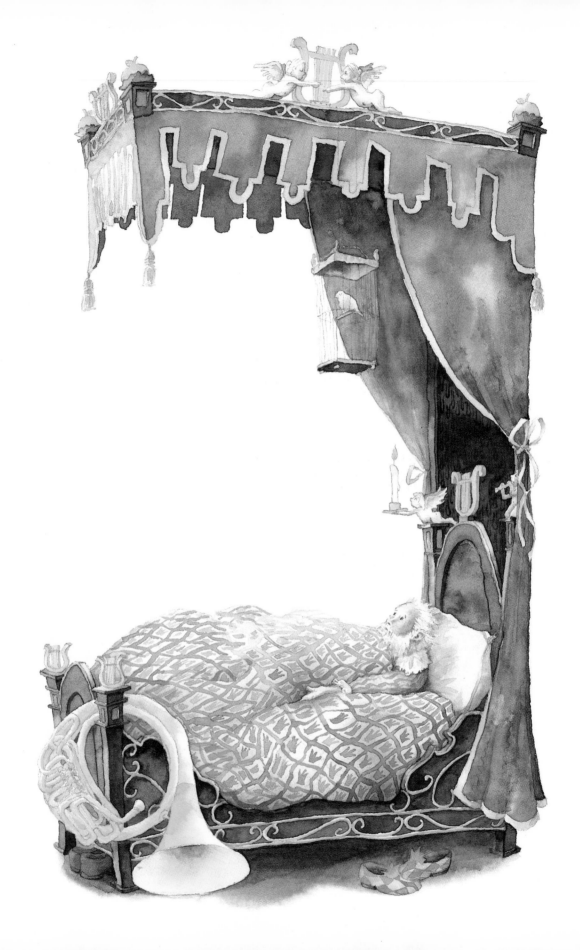

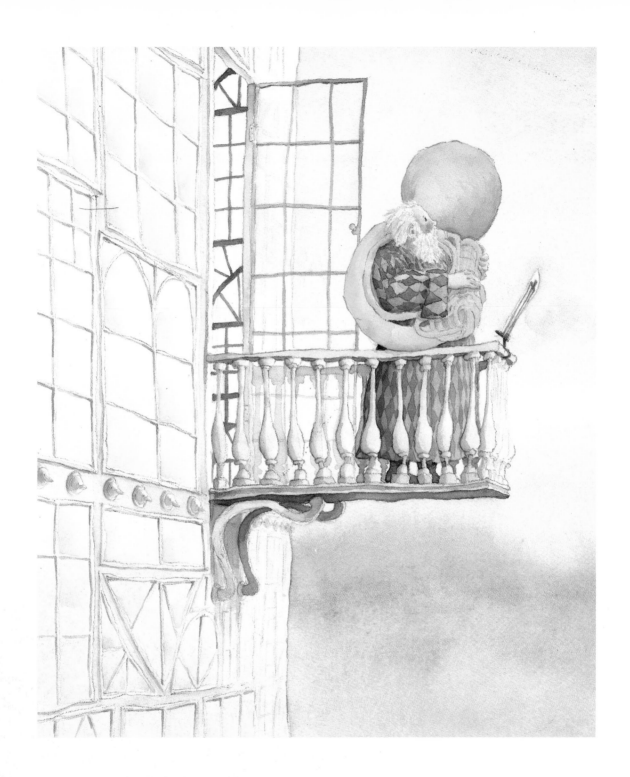

The old man lived in luxury. He ate only delicacies, he slept beneath eiderdown. He played for the entire city and could enjoy a new, breathtaking view every day.

He saw buildings with copper roofs, churches with pointed spires,
lovely landscaped parks with statues and fountains. And here and
there he saw people standing in line, lines that grew longer every
day. What could they be waiting for? What were they doing?
He became so curious that he finally went down to the city
to see for himself.

There he saw that people were waiting their turn
behind big telescopes angled — toward his palace!

The old man ran to the front of the line and pushed aside a boy who was gazing intently into the telescope. But once he saw what the boy had just seen, he became so upset that he walked straight to the King's palace.

"Your Majesty," he said. "Would you have those telescopes removed as soon as possible?"

"Removed?" asked the King, surprised.

"Everybody can see what happens in my palace."

"People are not harming you by looking, are they?"

"No, that's true," said the old man. "But would you please provide curtains?"

"Curtains for as many windows as there are days in a year?"

The old man realized that he had to live with people looking at him. But he couldn't.

He asked his servants to cover the windows. They hung sheets in front of them and tapestries and lengths of cloth, but it was hopeless. The old man didn't know which way to turn. At night he crawled deep down under his quilt; he built a wall of books around his plate when he ate; and he could no longer draw a single sound from his helicon. And although he had not yet set foot in the towers, he lacked the strength to climb all the way up.

Early one morning, he put on his clothes and crept out of the palace, down the mountain. The helicon rested like lead on his shoulders, and the city square had never seemed so immense.

When he finally reached the other side, he headed for the music
shop. But the sign was gone and the shop was empty.

He hung the helicon on the sign hook and rang the neighbor's bell.
A sleepy woman opened the door.

"Forgive me for waking you," said the old man. "Could you tell
me what happened to the music-shop owner and his little
daughter?"

"The poor child could not bear the sound of that instrument on
the mountain," said the woman. "Her little flute was drowned out
by it all the time. That's why they left."

"I see," said the old man, and he walked slowly away.
He was so bent over that he looked as if he was
still carrying the helicon.

The sun was beginning to set when he reached the village. In the marketplace, he heard someone playing the flute. He recognized the sounds, but he had never heard the melody before. He walked quietly toward the linden tree, and there he saw who was playing.

He waited until the tune was finished. Then he straightened his back and continued on his way. He walked through the village and down the green path which led home to his cottage.